S0-ANO-117

THE MOUNTAIN AND THE GOAT

SIAMAK TAGHADDOS

ILLUSTRATIONS BY:
ZACHARY CAIN

Poetti

First Edition

I ran and I ran
to the mountain, I ran.

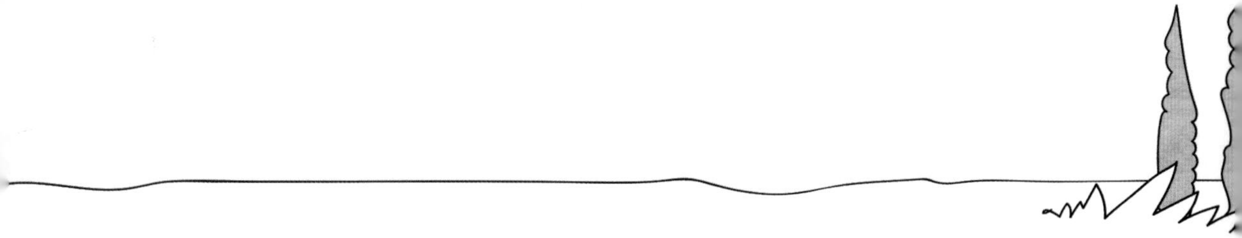

There I saw a goat who sang and sang.

"You're in luck!
Here's some water.
Here's some bread.

Do as you wish,
but plan ahead!"

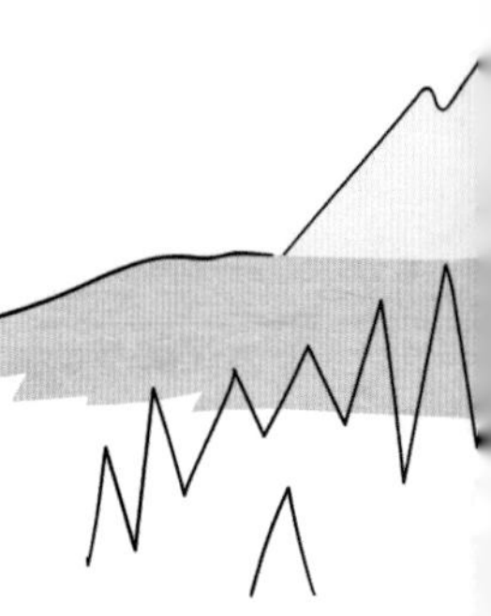

I ate the bread
and watered the soil.

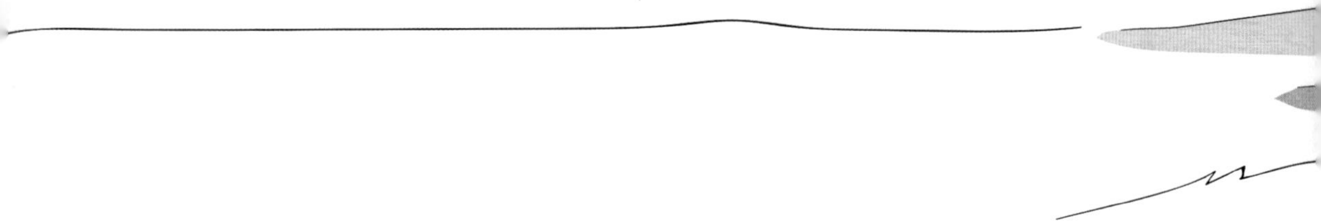

The soil gave me grass.

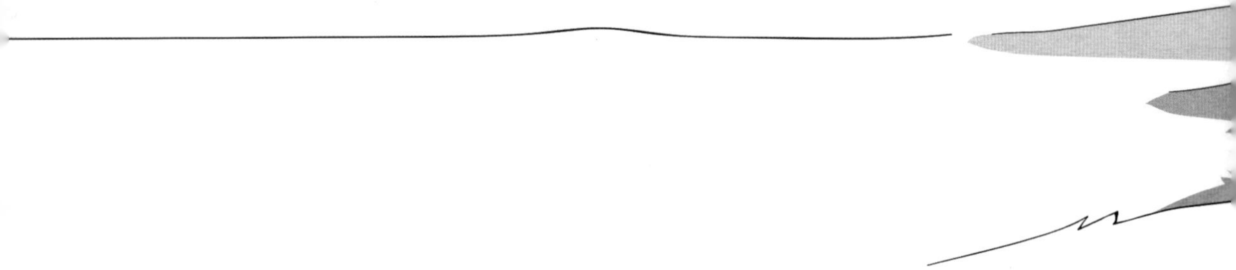

The grass I fed to the cow.

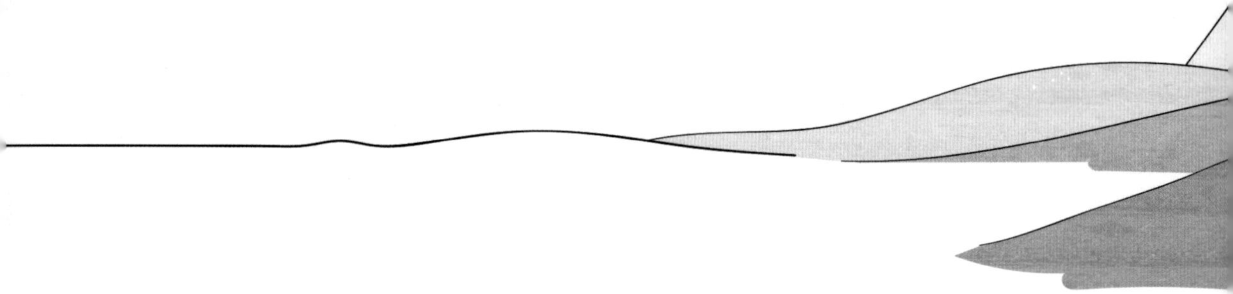

The cow gave me milk.

MiLK

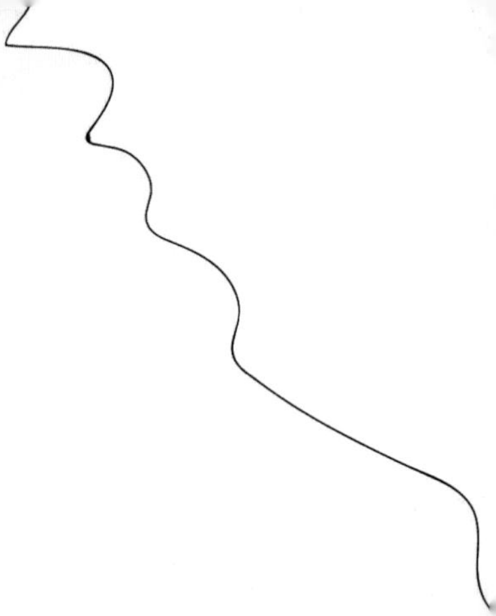

The milk I gave to the smith.

MILK

The smith gave me scissors.

MiLK

The scissors I gave to the tailor.

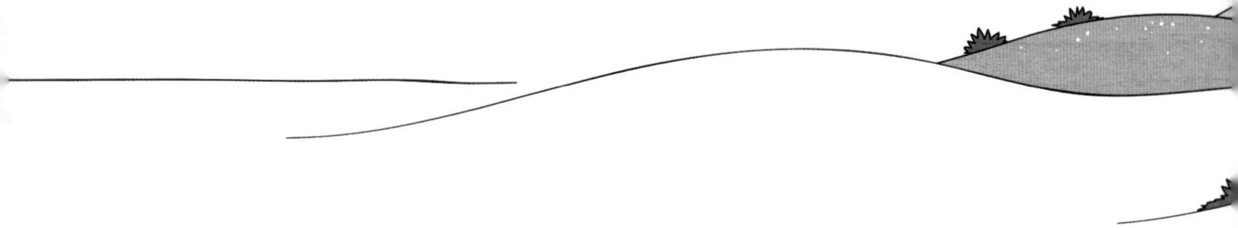

The tailor gave me a coat.

The coat I gave to the doctor.

E
F P
T O Z

The doctor gave me glasses.

E
F P
T O Z
L P E D

The glasses I gave to my dad.

My dad gave me lumber.

And together
we built a tree house.

And then we took a nap!

Illustrations by Zachary Cain.

Published by Poetti.

Las Vegas, Nevada.

poettibooks.com

ISBN 978-1-7342464-0-7

Library of Congress Control Number: 2019919217

Printed in China.

Poetti

THE MOUNTAIN AND THE GOAT